Monsieur Lambert

Jean-Jacques Sempé

Phaidon Press Limited
Regent's Wharf
All Saints Street
London N1 9PA

Phaidon Press Inc.
180 Varick Street
New York, NY 10014

www.phaidon.com

English Edition © 2006 Phaidon Press Ltd
First published in French as *Monsieur Lambert* by Éditions Denoël
© 1965 Sempé and Éditions Denoël

ISBN-13: 978 0 7148 4623 1
ISBN-10: 0 7148 4623 6

A CIP catalogue record for this book is available from the British Library.

Translated by Anthea Bell
Design concept adapted by Marianne Noble
Printed in China

Monsieur Lambert

Jean-Jacques Sempé

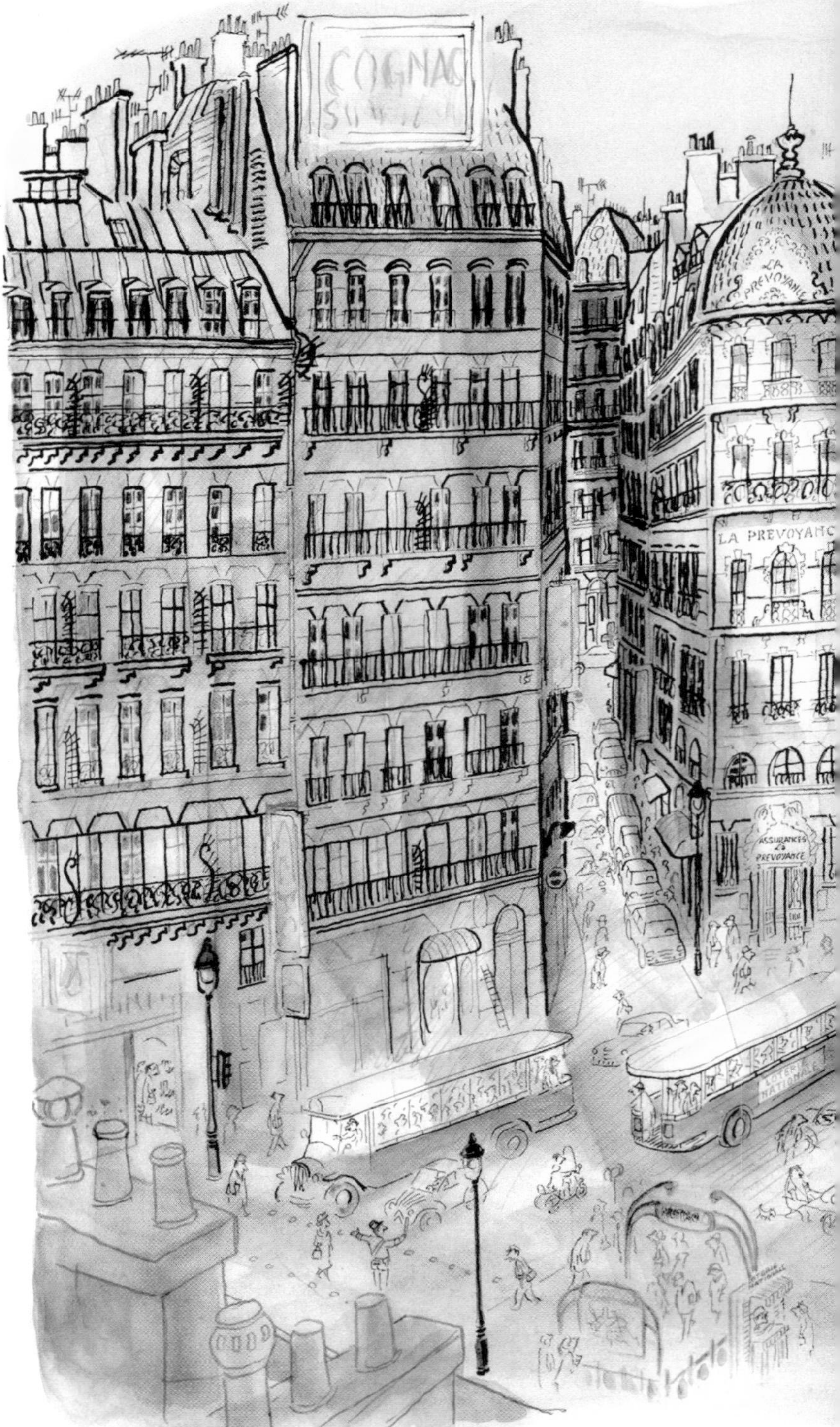
COGNAC
LA PREVOYANCE
LA PREVOYANC
ASSURANCES LA PREVOYANCE
LOTERIE NATIONALE

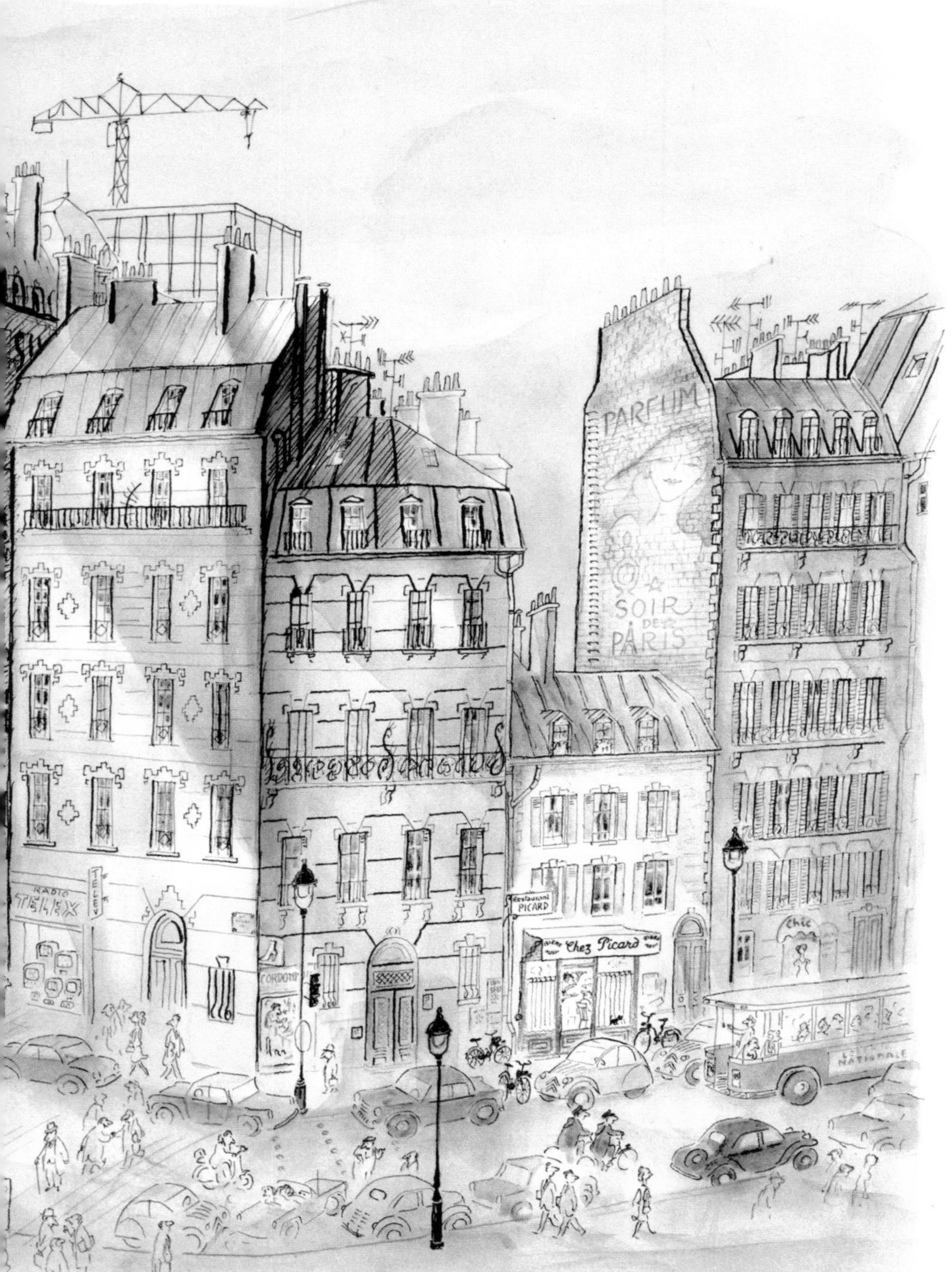
PARFUM
SOIR DE PARIS
RADIO
TELEX
Restaurant
PICARD
Chez Picard
Chic

Potage 0,80

service 10%

FERMÉ LE DIMANCHE

COUVERT 0,50
SERVIETTE Tissu 0,30
SERVIETTE Cellulose . 0,10

La Maison n'est pas responsable
des vêtements ou objets perdus,
échangés ou tachés.

VINS EN CARAFE

	carafe	carafon	verre
Rouge	1,10	0,75	0,45
Blanc	1,30	0,75	0,45
Rosé	1,60	0,90	0,50
Beaujolais	5	2,50	
Côtes-du-Rhône	4	2,30	1,10

	bout	1/2 bout
Bordeaux rouge	7,50	4
Chantegorge	4,50	
Rosé d'Anjou	4	2,35
Rosé de Provence	4	2,30
Alsace	5	2,75
Muscadet	4,25	2,75

BIÈRE
La bouteille 25 cl. .. 1....

CIDRE
La bouteille 25 cl. .. 1....

EAUX MINÉRALES

Vichy	1,10	0,60
Vittel	1,10	0,60
Perrier	1,20	0,70
Café express	0,60	
Infusions	0,80	

DEMANDEZ
LA CARTE DES VINS

Contenance de la verrerie :
Carafe 42 cl. - Carafon 21 cl.

RESTAURANT
CHEZ PICARD

MENU 12 Février 1965

Hors d'œuvres Crudités 1,30
saucisson sec 0,90
Carottes rapées 0,90
œuf dur mayonnaise 0,90

Plat du jour
Quart de poulet Bressoise 4,70 (Coq au vin
Supp¹ 0,90)
Steak purée 3,70
Saumon maître d'Hôtel 4,50

Légumes Purée 1,15 Pommes allumettes 1,30
salade de Laitue 1
chaux de Bruxelles 1,30

Fromages Camembert 0,90 Carré de l'est 0,90
port salut 1,10 Chèvre 1 Suisse 0,80 yaourt 0,60
Cantal 0,90 Roquefort 1,30 (beurre 0,10)
Supp¹

Desserts Tarte abricots 1,20 Compote 1,10
Fruit 1 gâteau de riz 0,90
confiture de cerise 0,90
crème caramel 1

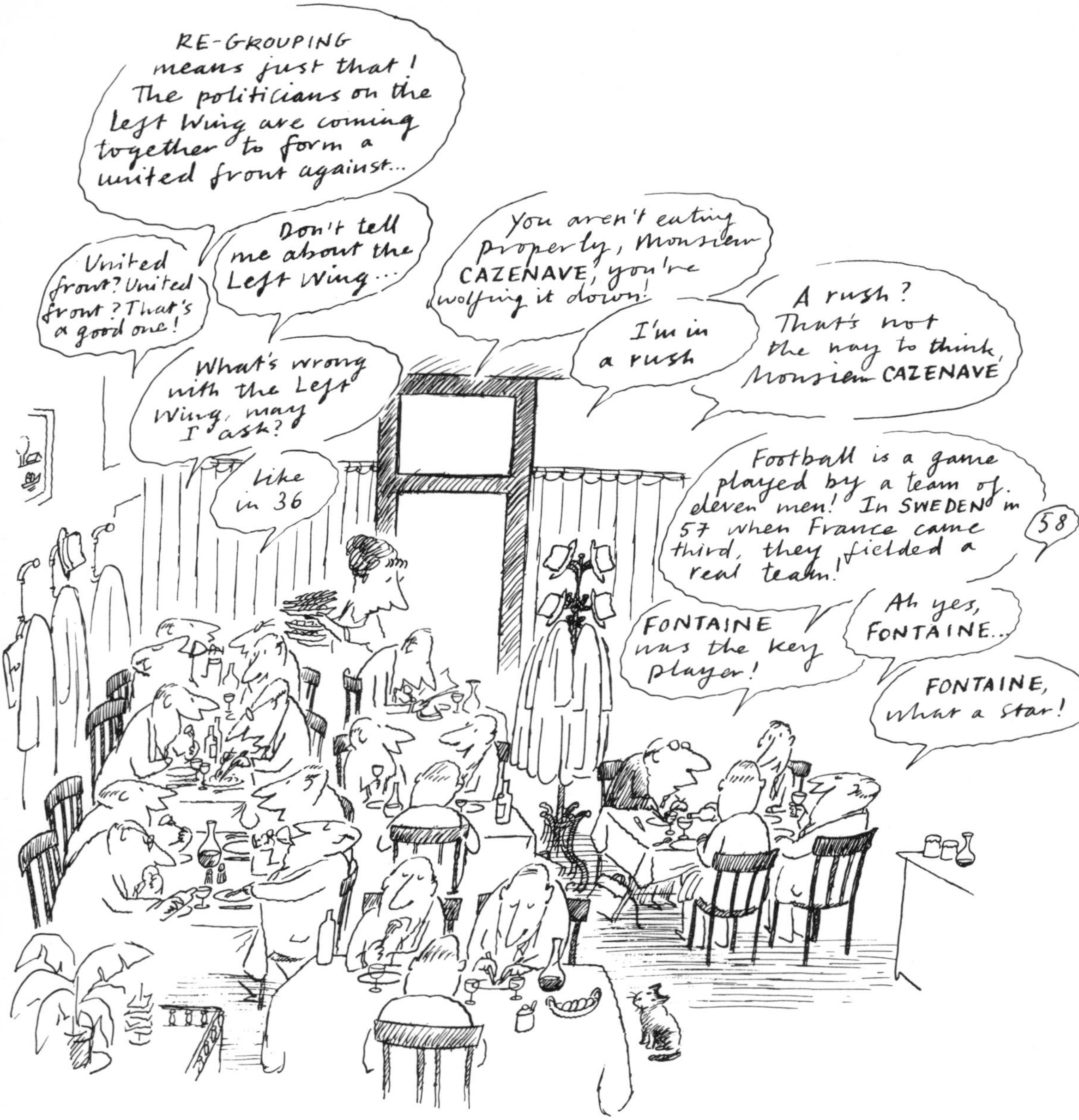
RE-GROUPING means just that! The politicians on the Left Wing are coming together to form a united front against...
United front? United front? That's a good one!
Don't tell me about the Left Wing...
What's wrong with the Left Wing, may I ask?
Like in 36
You aren't eating properly, Monsieur CAZENAVE, you're wolfing it down!
I'm in a rush
A rush? That's not the way to think, Monsieur CAZENAVE
Football is a game played by a team of eleven men! In SWEDEN in 57 when France came third, they fielded a real team!
58
FONTAINE was the key player!
Ah yes, FONTAINE...
FONTAINE, what a star!

Yesterday we had the chef's terrine, followed by bœuf à la mode or Wiener schnitzel with salad of the day. That's because it was Tuesday, and on Tuesday the menu is terrine, followed by bœuf à la mode or Wiener schnitzel with salad of the day ...

On Wednesday, we had the usual choice of celeriac rémoulade or mackerel in white wine followed by rabbit casserole, salad, cheese, Mont-Blanc pudding or the tart of the day, because that's Wednesday's usual menu. The unusual thing was that Lambert wasn't there, and it was almost half past one.

Of course Lambert's absence didn't go unnoticed. However, we were able to field the rather pointed questions easily enough ...

after all our little group is well known for its profoundly liberal attitude. This made us feel Lambert's worrying absence even more acutely.

We resumed our conversation. It was one thirty-five. Lambert had never been later than twelve thirty, or perhaps twenty to one. Chaudère had seen him on the Number 66 that morning, so he wasn't ill.

Lambert arrived at one forty. We just said hello as if nothing had happened.

Lambert gave no explanation. And we didn't ask him for one. Lambert is Lambert, and if he wants to arrive at twenty to two he can.

We also didn't ask him why he wasn't eating. He usually likes to eat his lunch while it's hot, but today his rabbit casserole was cooling on his plate (he had passed on the celeriac to save time).

We simply pointed out that it was getting cold.

Next day, Thursday (artichokes vinaigrette, leg of lamb with creamed potatoes or mixed beans), Lambert still wasn't there at one thirty.

He arrived between twenty and twenty-five to two, still looking odd.
We would sooner have bitten off our tongues than ask him any questions.

On Friday we were in for a big surprise. Lambert was there before everyone else. He was just finishing his hake meunière.

He gulped down his bleu d'Auvergne, refused pudding, and left.

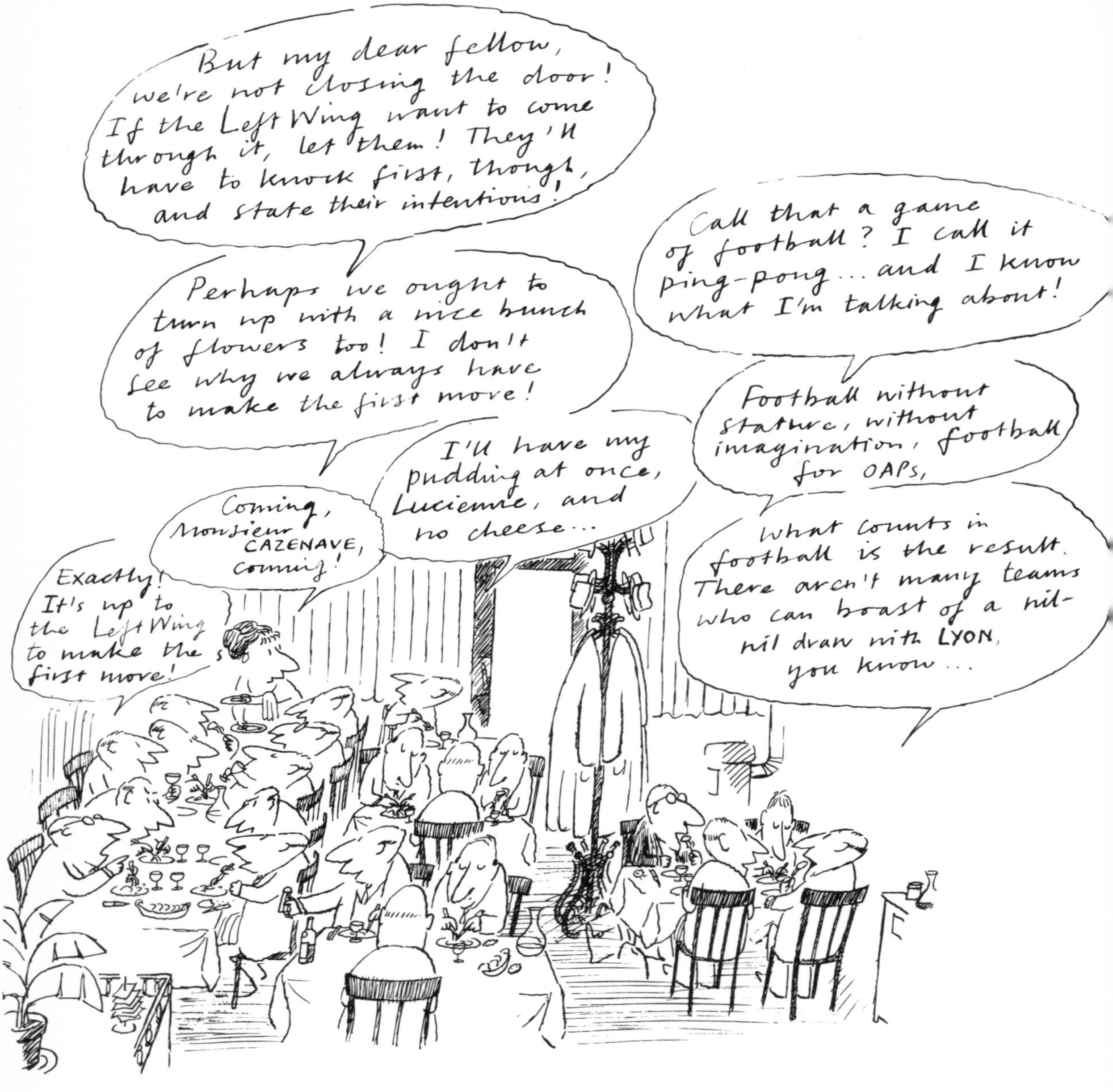

The following Monday, Lambert was there on time ...

but he was also somewhere else. Let me explain: he was there, but elsewhere; well, you understand, he wasn't there. He didn't really notice what he was eating, and didn't really join in the conversation. Of course we pretended not to notice Lambert's rather odd behaviour.

On Tuesday something apparently inconsequential happened. We were discussing I don't quite remember what, when Lambert suddenly spoke, making a comment, so we thought, about the terrine, which happened to be on his plate at the time.

We were quite taken aback. Usually he turns up his nose at the terrine,
and every Tuesday at the beginning of the month he chooses from
the à la carte menu instead – maybe chicory (he loves chicory), maybe
a palm-heart – but that wasn't to be the last surprise he sprang on us.

He didn't keep us waiting. He spoke frankly. He'd met a woman.
A wonderful woman. Now that he had let the cat out of the bag, he
was going to tell us everything: why he sometimes arrived at twenty
to two, and why he sometimes left at half past twelve. It would
explain everything.

Her name was FLORENCE. He described her in detail. She was the really womanly type. Woman with a capital W. The kind of woman that every man instantly recognizes.

From then on everything was different. On the days when Lambert wasn't there when we arrived (and he never warned us – perhaps he didn't want to or perhaps he didn't know in advance if he'd be seeing Florence), we made the most of his absence.

We relived our dreams and memories of past love. When one of us came back down to earth, it was to share a snippet from their love life.

And of course we had all had many amorous adventures. Some exciting, some thrilling, others frankly incredible. In short, we had lived life to the full,

which is why we could totally understand Lambert and even advise him. He was young, and of course he didn't yet have the sophistication you need for a love affair in the grand style.

Then Lambert would arrive. His love life was complicated. She took the Number 95. He caught the Number 66 at five past eight so he could meet her at the Havre-Caumartin stop – even though the eight-sixteen would have been more convenient. Then he got on the Number 95 that she was on and went as far as Palais-Royal with her …

they got out, walked a little way together, and then he took the Number 39 to Sentier and reached his office just on time. They would meet between twelve and two, sometimes before and sometimes after lunch, for an aperitif or a coffee. He managed to see her for a few moments in the evening too.

One day, by ten to two Lambert still hadn't arrived. We were very concerned: maybe Florence hadn't turned up, and he was waiting for her until the last minute. We went back to work, but our hearts weren't in it.

Next day Lambert was back. The day before had been a red-letter day:
he'd invited Florence out to lunch. We could tell that everything had
gone very, very well. We all agreed to order from the à la carte menu
(the coq au vin), and we finished lunch with a small armagnac.

We saw Lambert less and less often, only two or three times a week, when with the discretion of a true gentleman he told us about his romance. What a lucky man!

We now knew all about each other's love lives. Chaudère had loved and been loved in return. Some women had mattered a lot, others less so, of course. Life, he acknowledged, had been good to him. In fact life had been good to all of us ...

Of course we at the bistro realized that Lambert was leading a rather exotic life, but we never referred to it, avoiding the subject with the delicacy of true friends.

Good old Lambert, it was his turn now. May he have as good a time as we once did.

Now, when Lambert turned up, we welcomed him with comments that sometimes made him blush with pleasure, or shyness, we didn't know which.

When he left, similar comments followed him.

Once he turned up with a tie we had never seen before. Florence, surely.

Another time he came in and an uproar ensued: he had lipstick on his left cheek.

How it happened I don't know, but we found ourselves talking at length about complications in our love lives that might have had disastrous consequences. All four of us were late back to the office.

One day, it was a Wednesday, we were analysing our greatest passion, in fact our only passion, our all-consuming passion: women.

Our friend Lambert arrived between twelve twenty-five or twelve thirty. We were not expecting him. He didn't look too good. He seemed to be in a bad mood. In fact, more than that, he looked sad, sad and disillusioned ...

He sat down. We asked no questions. As it was Wednesday, we ate our asparagus, our rabbit casserole, and so on ...

Over the next few days Lambert was back with us. Turning up on the dot, the way he did *before*. We tried to engage him in various topics of conversation, to drive away the black thoughts that made him look so sad.

We picked up the threads of our lives again. Lambert said little,
but we knew our friendship did him good. Because with men,
it's friendship that counts. Friendship matters more than anything.
As everyone knows, all life's troubles are caused by women.

We knew that he was grateful to us for being so tactful. We weren't
going to pester him with questions or advice ...

We hoped he would recover. With the help of his friends he would recover, and sooner than *she* thought. You should not allow women to become too important in your life – not that any of us ever had.

There are some men who regret not having known many women.
For us that's not the case. The other day Chaudère was saying,
"I never cared for women. One or two incidents really put me off."
And Chaudère is right.

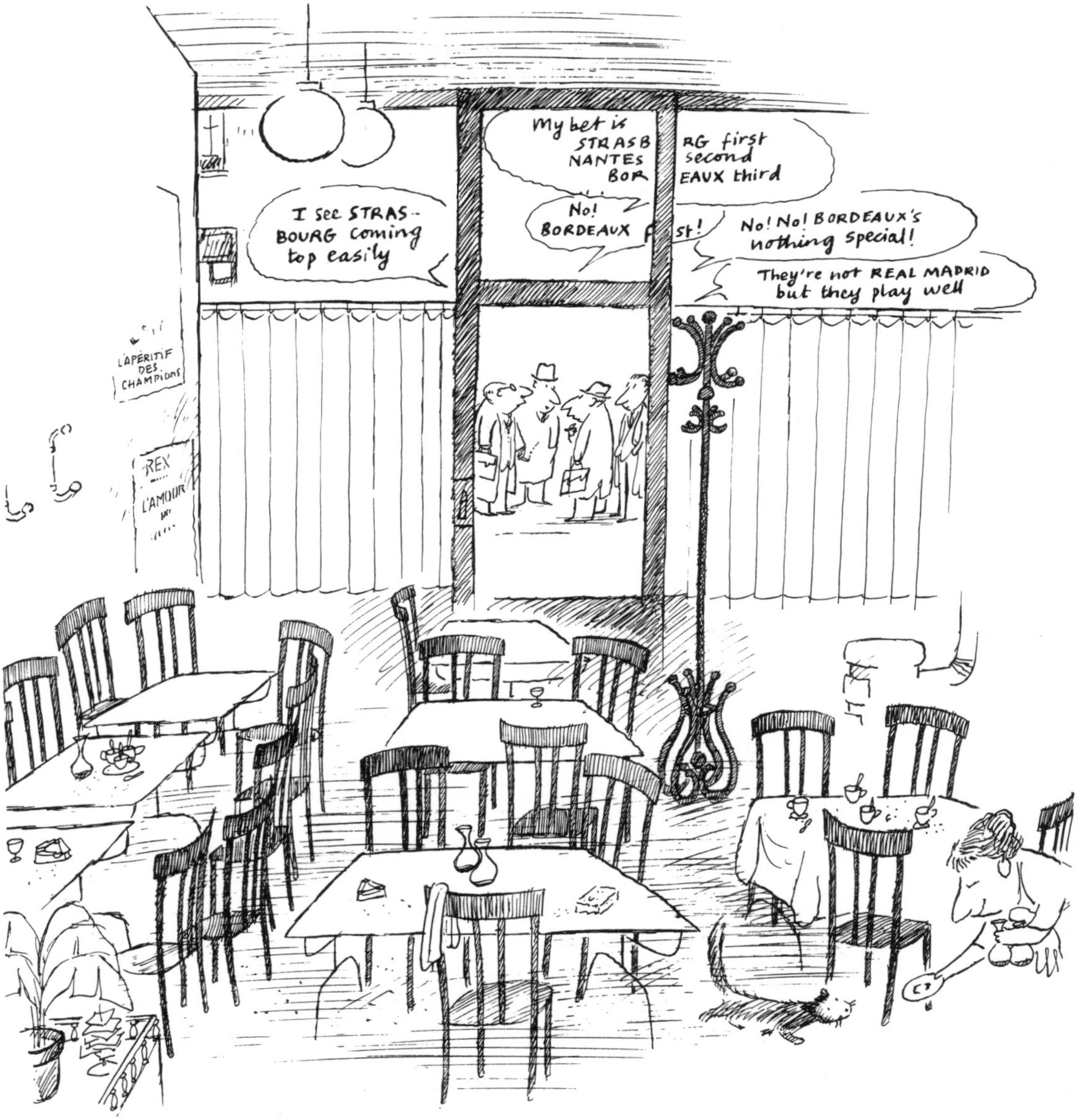
I see STRAS-BOURG coming top easily
My bet is STRASB RG first NANTES second BOR EAUX third
No! BORDEAUX f st!
No! No! BORDEAUX's nothing special!
They're not REAL MADRID but they play well
L'APÉRITIF DES CHAMPIONS
REX
L'AMOUR

There's one thing we've always been passionate about: football. We all used to play. We thought nothing of women compared to football. And we still don't. When compared with football, women meant nothing. They still don't.

Football has always been our life. It's the team spirit that matters (women know nothing about team spirit). Football is eleven good mates who enjoy getting together for a game.

It's a bit like us. We enjoy getting together for lunch every day. From Monday to Friday. On Monday it's leek vinaigrette, steak and chips, rice pudding ...

On Tuesday it's the chef's terrine and bœuf à la mode or Wiener schnitzel. And today is Tuesday, it's a quarter to two and Lambert still isn't here. What a devil. He really has a roving eye! Well, he's right to have fun. You must have fun while you're young. And we'd be the last to begrudge him that.

The
End.

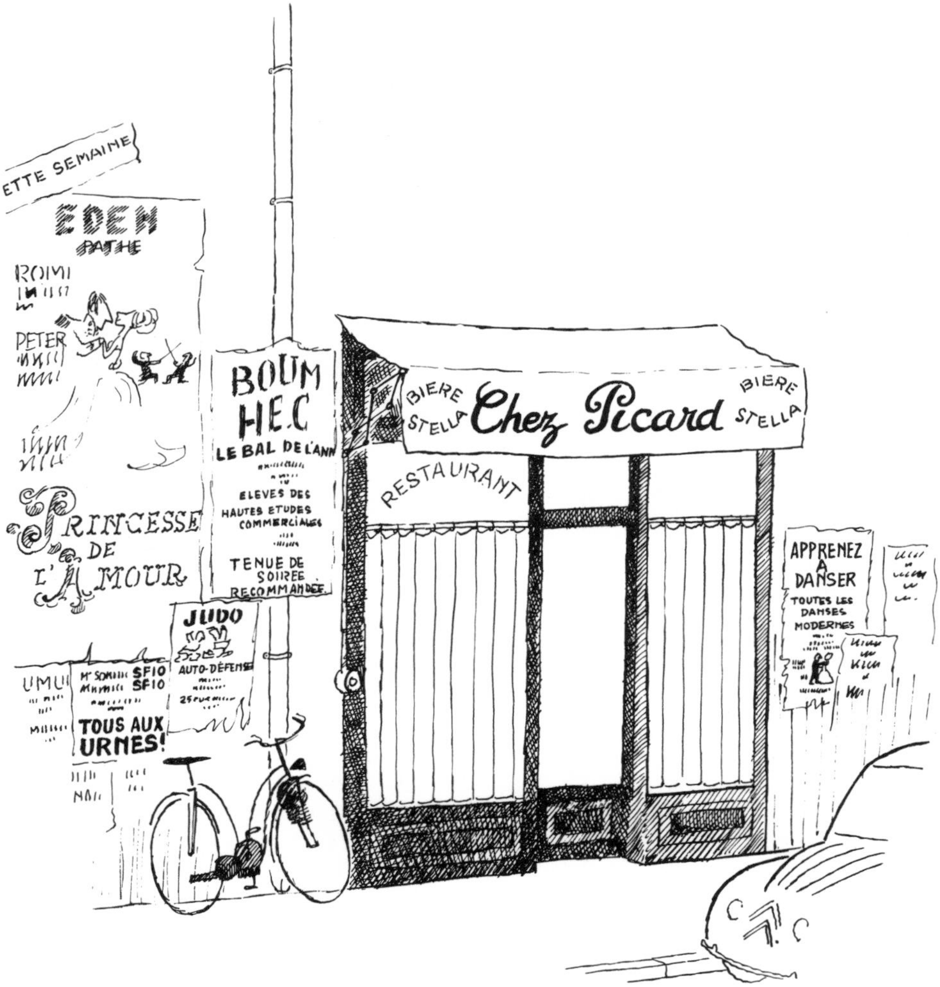
ETTE SEMAINE
EDEN
PATHE
ROMI
PETER
PRINCESSE DE L'AMOUR
BOUM
HE.C
LE BAL DE L'ANN
ELEVES DES HAUTES ETUDES COMMERCIALES
TENUE DE SOIREE RECOMMANDÉE
JUDO
AUTO-DÉFENSE
SFIO
SFIO
TOUS AUX URNES!
BIERE STELLA
Chez Picard
BIERE STELLA
RESTAURANT
APPRENEZ A DANSER
TOUTES LES DANSES MODERNES

Potage 0,70

service 15%

FERMÉ LE DIMANCHE

COUVERT 0,50
SERVIETTE Tissu 0,30
SERVIETTE Cellulose . 0,10

La Maison n'est pas responsable
des vêtements ou objets perdus,
échangés ou tachés.

VINS EN CARAFE

	carafe	carafon	verre
Rouge	1,10	0,70	0,55
Blanc	1,30	0,70	0,45
Rosé	1,60	0,90	0,50
Beaujolais	5	2,90	
Côtes-du-Rhône	4	2,30	1,10

	bout.	1 2 bout.
Bordeaux rouge	4,60	2,70
Chantegorge	4,80	
Rosé d'Anjou		
Rosé de Provence	4	2,30
Alsace	5	
Muscadet	4,40	2,75

BIÈRE
La bouteille 25 cl. . 1 .....

CIDRE
La bouteille 25 cl. . 1 .....

EAUX MINÉRALES
Vichy ... 1,10 ... 0,60 ...
Vittel ... 1,10 ... 0,60 ...
Perrier . 1,20 ... 0,70 ...
Café express ... 0,60 ...
Infusions ...... 0,90 ...

DEMANDEZ
LA CARTE DES VINS

Contenance de la verrerie :
Carafe 42 cl. - Carafon 21 cl.

RESTAURANT
CHEZ PICARD

MENU 15 Mars 1965

Hors d'œuvre
Céleri rémoulade 1,40
Maquereau vin blanc 1,40
Carottes râpées 0,80
Saucisson sec ou ail 0,90

Plat du jour
Lapin chasseur 4,90
Côte de porc lentilles 4,20
Tournedos garni 4,20
Colin beurre fondu 3,90 (à l'Américaine supp⁰ 1.30)

Légumes Purée 1,20 Pommes allumettes 1,30
salade de saison 0,90

Fromages Camembert 0,90 Carré de l'Est 0,90
chèvre 1 Suisse 0,80 yaourt 0,60
Bleu d'Auvergne 1,30 livarot 1,30

Desserts Mont Blanc 1,20 Tarte Maison 1,20
Menthient 0,90 gâteau aux amandes 1,30